# THE GOOD

ROBBIE KILDAIRE

From my class

KEIRA HAMILTON

My best friend

CHELSEA DOYLE

BRILLIANT actress

# THE ANNOYING

TOBY PIRANHA

TV Producer

MUM

Need I say more?

LUCY LIONS

Assistant Producer

VANILLA MOONFIRE

Life Coach and Spiritual ~~Emmp~~ Empath

HARRY HEATHCLIFFE

The horriblest boy at school

**MY TOTALLY SECRET DIARY: REALITY TV NIGHTMARE**
A RED FOX BOOK 978 1 862 30424 6

First published in Great Britain by Doubleday,
an imprint of Random House Children's Books
A Random House Group Company

Doubleday edition published 2010
Red Fox edition published 2012

1 3 5 7 9 10 8 6 4 2

Text and illustrations copyright © Dee Shulman, 2010

The Random House Group Limited supports the Forest Stewardship Council (FSC®),
the leading international forest certification organization. Our books carrying the FSC
label are printed on FSC®-certified paper. FSC is the only forest certification scheme
endorsed by the leading environmental organizations, including Greenpeace.
Our paper procurement policy can be found at www.**randomhouse**.co.uk/environment.

Text handwritten by Dee Shulman

Red Fox Books are published by Random House Children's Books,
61–63 Uxbridge Road, London W5 5SA

www.**kidsatrandomhouse**.co.uk
www.**totallyrandombooks**.co.uk
www.**randomhouse**.co.uk

Addresses for companies within The Random House Group Limited can be found at:
www.**randomhouse**.co.uk/offices.htm

THE RANDOM HOUSE GROUP Limited Reg. No. 954009

A CIP catalogue record for this book is available from the British Library.

Printed and bound in Singapore

# My
# TOTALLY SECRET
## Diary

**Reality TV Nightmare**

I am **NOT** ~~exaj~~ exaggerating

Belonging entirely to me,
↓

## Polly Price

So PLEASE RETURN IT TO ME A.S.A.P. (or Sooner)

Dee Shulman

# FRIDAY May 16th   8.15 am

A few minutes ago, I was **trying** to crunch my way through a bowlful of totally **HEALTHY** (horrible) cereal.

As each spoonful takes about **300** chews, I had <u>plenty</u> of time to read the back of the box.

| INGREDIENTS |
| --- |
| SPELT FLAKES |
| AMARANTH SEEDS |
| RAW PEPITAS |
| ORGANIC QUINOA |
| AGAVE NECTAR |
| MACA |
| CHILEAN FLAME RAISINS |
| MEDJOOL DATES |

? → AMARANTH SEEDS
?? → ORGANIC QUINOA
??? → MACA

I was <u>hoping</u> to find some sort of TOXIC ingredient

*Like sugar or caramel*

so I could ~~perswade~~ ~~pursu~~ persuade Mum it <u>wasn't</u> healthy and could we please, please, **PLEASE** get some cocoa-pops.

3

...Karzee...Deringa... Meningkana. Chang...

...Kama

But it's impossible to ~~consontrate~~ concentrate on even the _easiest_ job when your mother is CHANTING!

...Nicardonga - Chimichanga...

Then the phone rang. It was right next to Mum so I ignored it.

So did she.

Then her mobile started to ring.

Hmph.

I kindly picked it up and took it over to her. She ignored me _and_ the phone. So I put it on the floor beside her, and went back to my delicious breakfast.

# AGGHHH!!!

## THIS will be a TOTAL DISASTER!

EVERYBODY watches Celebrity Home Watch.

That means everybody at school will see it...

Kenwood High
(My school)

KENWOOD HIGH SCHOOL

↑ ↑ ↑ ↑
Keira Me Ellie Jo

My Mum- (The Actress)

...where they don't even know about Mum...

... And I HAVE to keep it that way.

Mum being on Celebrity Home Watch would mean Charlie Bonnyface, the TV presenter, coming to our house with a load of cameras and filming EVERYTHING that happens!

7.15 pm CELEBRITY HOME WATCH  C7

Who will be Charlie's celebrity victim tonight?

Arabella
Diamonte

LOVE
LINGERS

If the kids at school get to watch that, my life will be OVER.

While all these dark thoughts were running through my head I promised Sonia Snootwhistle that I'd tell Mum (as soon as she returned from whichever planet she'd gone to).

CHAKKA-RA
KOOLINGA......

Planet Mum

Then I paced.

I needed a strategy.

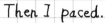

But the only strategy I could come up with was to <u>not</u> <u>tell</u> Mum her agent had rung.

Well <u>obviously.</u>

But what if Sonia rang back when I was at school?

How could I stop Mum answering the phone?..

I needed a <u>proper</u> plan.

The only way I can ever come up with a proper plan is to write stuff down. So I spent 10 minutes <u>trying</u> to find a piece of paper (the pc printer was empty as usual.)

And then I remembered **THIS NOTEBOOK!**

I **LOVE** the cover, but why would you put a cover like that on a maths exercise book?

Maybe for a disguise?

Maybe to make someone think maths is fun?

Anyway I know it's a really **ancient** notebook, because I'd rescued it from the bottom of a box of **ancient** stuff Mum was throwing out.

I think it may be from France, because there was an ~~anteek~~ antique ticket inside it.

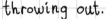

~~Dok~~ Document attached ➡

It could be a family ~~airloom~~ heirloom? Must remember to ask Mum.

UH-OH! She has stopped droning — gotta hide this book. If she sees it I AM <u>DEAD</u>.

ST4   37   14 B

PARIS VISITE
CARTE N° 4936-2
2 CL   3 JOURS   ZONES   1 à 5
DU 03/02/98
AU 06/02/98
51338

## LATER   At School

(History Lesson — we're supposed to be watching a film about the Fire of London, but it's dark so Mr Edwards can't see me writing)

This is what happened when Mum stopped chanting.

Darling — who was on the phone?

Er — can't remember...

<u>Why</u> did I say that?

<u>Why</u> didn't I say it was my friend Keira from school? Or Aunty Kate?

Hyppolita! You are the daughter of an actress! You do <u>NOT</u> forget who you received phone calls from. You write down messages! You write down names. You write down phone numbers. The phone is my Doorway to Opportunity! How many times do you need to be told? Now **THINK!** Who-was-on-the-phone?

I just stood there. I couldn't quite bring myself to actually lie. And I couldn't quite bring myself to tell the truth.

Then 2 things happened. The doorbell and the phone rang at the same time. — DING DONG

I dived for the phone

BRING!!

Mum got there first. →

My heart sank.

Celebrity Home Watch? ME? Oh Sonia, that's wonderful! When?..MONDAY?..But it's Friday today! That's impossible! Of course I'm not turning this down, but you'll just have to get back on the phone and tell them Arabella Diamonte needs time to prepare...Oh for goodness sake, Sonia — what do I care about production schedules? Just get them to delay it —

The doorbell rang again and I trudged over to answer it.

You ready, Poll?

Keira Hamilton—
my best friend

OH NO!!!

Mr Edwards is comi

POLLY PRICE!

LATER - about 4.30pm

OK! As if my life wasn't bad enough, I've now got a ~~detenshon~~ detention from Mr Edwards.

The only good thing is I managed to ~~conseal~~ hide this diary before he got to my desk. So I only got my detention for lack of ~~consontration~~ concentration.

But how can you be expected to ~~consontrate~~ concentrate on history when your LIFE _is about to end?_

On the way home, Keira kept stopping.

Look – what's wrong?

_Obviously_ I couldn't tell her. But she was coming home with me for tea, so how could I keep her from finding out?

AGGHH!

The only thing that kept me putting one foot in front of the other was the teeny weeny hope that Mum had managed to put them off filming her altogether.

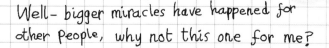

Absolutely not! I couldn't possibly be filmed then... I need WEEKS to prepare...

Well– bigger miracles have happened for other people, why not this one for me?

13

I was just about to put my key in the lock, when the front door opened and this...this... ~~aperish apperit~~ APPARITION was standing there.

You must be the child.

Who are YOU?

HYPPOLITA!-

My shoes were whooshed from my feet, and the front door was shut.

SLAM

MUM! Keira was supposed to be coming for tea!

How long?

How long is it, Vanilla?

I think in **real** time it's three weeks, but in **Cosmic** time, it has been an **ETERNITY!** We have known each other since before time began!

Oh Vanilla, so beautifully expressed!

I am here to help your mother prepare for the ~~inva~~ imminent invasion! I have of course put aside all other demands in order to channel my **FOCUS** and **POWERS** here.

Your **focus** and **powers**?

Sounds like she's been reading too much Harry Potter.

We have to begin with the house. And then we can move on to you and your mother. But time is short, so if you will excuse us... Are you ready, Arabella? We're just off to buy some fish.

FISH?

They've gone.

17

I thought they were supposed to be cleansing the house!

Anyway I hate fish...

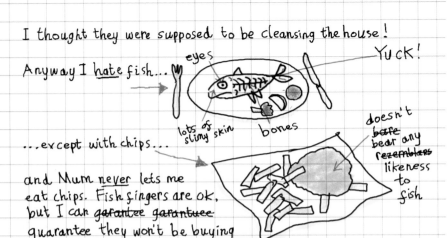

Yuck!

eyes

lots of slimy skin

bones

doesn't ~~bare~~ bear any ~~rezemblers~~ likeness to fish

...except with chips...

and Mum _never_ lets me eat chips. Fish fingers are ok, but I can ~~garantee garantuee~~ guarantee they won't be buying fish fingers. Not _healthy_ or _organic_ enough.

So Keira was LUCKY she got un-invited. She just texted to say her dad's taking them all to Pizza World...

SIGH!

Uh-Oh! Mum's back.

Polly! Polly-Pop! Come and see!

Why would she want me to come and look at her shopping?

## A BIT LATER

Well—I got that wrong.
It was _fish_ fish!

We've <u>never</u> been allowed pets before! I can't think how Vanilla managed to get Mum to agree! They're BEAUTIFUL!

But then Vanilla wouldn't let us put the fish tank down anywhere.

> No, no, my lambs. The water needs space around it for the energy to collect and connect! Let me stand here for a moment and feel the energy channels— Mmmmmm m mmmm mmmmmmm ... Perhaps here? Maybe not.

About **an hour** later, after following Vanilla around the house as she searched for the—er—

> Mmm-richest energy field...

> hmmm...

> Mmmmmm...

> VANILLA! Decide NOW!

She FINALLY made her decision.

So I spent a pleasant half-hour staring into the fish tank, (which is now where the TV was)...

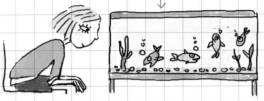

...while Mum and Vanilla kept themselves busy...
RUINING our house.

DOWNSTAIRS

## Living Room

The TV has now been moved miles away from the nearest chair— and for some reason is covered with a plastic tablecloth.

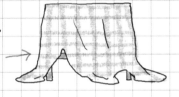

All the other furniture has been moved into the centre of the room, or removed altogether. (This includes my favourite squishy TV-watching chair.)

But, ~~spooky~~ spookiest of all, is the COFFEE-TABLE TRANSFORMATION

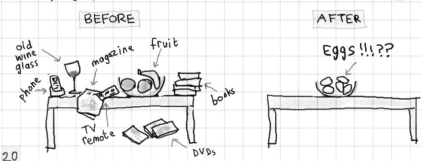

BEFORE

old wine glass
phone
magazine
fruit
TV remote
books
DVDs

AFTER

Eggs !!!??

# Dining Room

The table we eat off has been dragged out of its corner and is now taking up most of the room, and in the...

## Hall —conveniently placed right next to the front door—

there's a FOUNTAIN!

Aaghh! What's that doing there?

Even Mum seems vaguely surprised

## Mum's Inner ~~Sanktem~~ Sanctum

Have no idea what this means - but it's basically the room I'm not ~~aloud~~ allowed into.

### New additions

sparkly crystal hanging on red ribbon

picture of... EGGS

pile of red...EGGS

Yet another fountain!

desk moved to middle of floor

I decided to venture no further upstairs. It was _too_ _dangerous_.

PLUS the Vanilla Smile was getting creepy.

I went back downstairs, dragged a chair over to the telly and got under the plastic tablecloth with it.

A chance to forget my troubles for a few minutes...

Yeah, right!

Celebrity Home Watch was on.

And it was _impossible_ to hear anything on TV with all the noise of moving furniture upstairs.

WHAT ARE THEY DOING UP THERE? They'd better not have gone into my room.

23

## SATURDAY MORNING   May 17th

I was in too much ~~dispair~~ despair to write anything last night. I would have probably torn a hole in the page.

It's ~~OUTRAJ~~ ~~OUTRAGOUS~~ OUTRAGEOUS!

blank wall!

① They've taken down all my pictures! →

② They've moved my bed!

③ They've put a <u>stupid</u> windchime by my window so it makes a horrible noise all night!  →

CLUNK CLATTER

④ They've taken down my mirror and put it in a place where you can't stand in front of it!

⑤ And my desk is sitting on the <u>landing</u>!

⑥   IT's **MY** BEDROOM!!!!

I tried to ask Mum what was going on...

← outraged expression

I'll explain later, darling— I've got a migraine coming on!

The only bit of good news is that Vanilla finally went home, and the racket stopped.

Think I'll fight my way through the bamboo and water to get some breakfast.

A BIT LATER

THIS IS NOW ~~OFFISH~~ OFFICIALLY AND TOTALLY THE WORST DAY EVER OF MY WHOLE LIFE.

~~Vanilla Cruella~~ Godzilla has just arrived with...

3...

4... suitcases

1...

2...

And - I almost can't bring myself to write this... Mum has said she can move into...

... MY ROOM

Even I would never have guessed my mother could be so HEARTLESS. How could any mother do something so-so- TOTALLY mean? Is it legal to make your child homeless?

I bet it isn't.

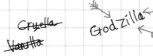

~~Cruella~~
~~Vanilla~~        Godzilla

25

When I asked very reasonably

Well - where am I supposed to sleep?

She actually TOLD ME OFF!

Oh Polly - do get that horrible tone out of your voice. How unwelcome you must be making Vanilla feel! You will be perfectly snug - I'm clearing you a space in my wardrobe.

This **HAS** to be child abuse! Surely?

I mean your Mum's wardrobe must be worse than The Cupboard Under the Stairs?

In fact I should probably stop writing and ring an organization that will come and rescue me. Right now...

Only... I don't know any.

And obviously I can't ask Mum. Or Vanilla.

And-well-
if I'm <u>totally</u>
honest, I have
to admit that
Mum's wardrobe
isn't <u>exactly</u> a
wooden
cupboard. →

It is in fact the size of a normal room. Actually it <u>was</u> a
normal room - the spare room - until Mum ran out of
space for her clothes in all the normal wardrobes.

But where am I
← supposed to fit in
it now?

I'm too ~~demorra~~
~~demoralised~~ fed up
to consider this
question, so I'm
going to phone
Keira and see if
I can go round to
hers.

Not very good photo - taken on my phone

# SATURDAY NIGHT May 17th

KEIRA

At least if you have a family that doesn't care about you at all, it's good to know that you have a friend who doesn't ask too many questions about why you're so ~~desparate~~ desperate to get away from your family.

And a friend's mother who cooks decent food, and lets you watch TV as long as you like. I wish I lived at Keira's.

We watched **SISTERS** (I love this programme - it's about 2 sisters, Jade and Jocasta, who have magical powers, but Mum says it's rubbish, and never lets me watch it!)

Then...

**6.30 pm  SISTERS   C5**

Jade (Chelsea Doyle) confronts warlock, Caen, (Bruce Ellis) in yet another fight against the Dark Forces.

...**MATCHMAKER** (quite annoying woman who tries to get girls and boys to fall in love but normally fails) and...

**7.30 pm  MATCHMAKER   C7**

Will they find love tonight?

28

... CELEBRITY HISSY FIT (really funny programme where they show famous people screaming and shouting and totally losing it - usually at photographers)

**8.15 pm CELEBRITY HISSY FIT** *MCB 4*

A chance to revel in maximum celebrity discomfort.

Keira's dad dropped me home, and I crept up to bed as Mum and Vanilla were chanting.

NIKAWAA WAAH HH

## SUNDAY MORNING May 18th

It turns out that Vanilla has a son! Do I feel sorry for him!

Anyway he is a PERSONAL TRAINER. And Vanilla has told my mum that she needs a Personal Trainer, as well as a Life Coach. So Vanilla's son is coming.

I have no idea what a Personal Trainer does, but if anyone can train my mother it would be a <u>good</u> thing.

HORRIBLE THOUGHT!!!
He may be just like Vanilla!

NIKAW BLAH BLAH!

29

## LATER

I now know what PERSONAL TRAINER means:

It means ...    PERSONAL ~~TORCHERER~~ TORTURER ← in the exercise department

That means he's like the
<u>worst</u> PE teacher you
ever had, but with only
<u>YOU</u> in the class!

massive ~~mussels~~ muscles

stop watch

evil grin

whistle

Also I don't remember hearing
Vanilla saying that <u>I</u> needed
a Personal Trainer.
And that's because <u>I</u> **DON'T.**

So why did <u>I</u> get forced
to go on a run round
the park with **ARIZONA**
and my mum?

I think
these legs
may be
battery-
powered.

Is this the name
of a normal
human being?
I don't think so.

30

The worst part of the whole thing was that Mum insisted on dressing the part.

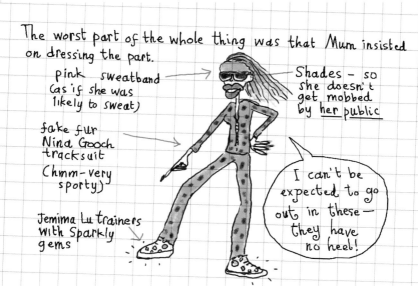

pink sweatband (as if she was likely to sweat)

Shades - so she doesn't get mobbed by her public

fake fur Nina Gooch tracksuit (hmm - very sporty)

Jemima Lu trainers with sparkly gems

I can't be expected to go out in these - they have no heel!

Then - just in case my day wasn't bad enough, on our way out, we got spotted by...

TOOT TOOT!

HARRY HEATHCLIFFE the totally HORRIBLE boy next door

Great look, POLLY-WALLY

Harry Heathcliffe's in the year above me at school. Most kids in the year above ignore me. Unfortunately he doesn't.

He followed us for a while, but finally got bored and went home. This was a good thing for 2 reasons:

1) He didn't witness my mum's totally embarrassing efforts at running... ↓

2) He wouldn't have much to report at school tomorrow.

But how was I going to stop him seeing the cameras when they showed up? Agghhh!

Anyway by some miracle we managed to limp round the park and home again without being recognized by anyone else.

As soon as she got in the front door,
Mum put her stilettos back on.

Tracky and high heels – not a good look →

Ahh! That's better!

But Arizona's mission wasn't over.

The best cardiovascular
blah blah blah is skipping. Aha yes!
Something you used to do in
the playground...

smug Vanilla-like smile

...So out into the garden,
both of you.

Mum refused to take her heels off.

Of course I can skip in heels –
I could walk a tightrope in heels...

Actually she couldn't skip in heels. On her first jump she
got the rope trapped under the heel
and fell over.

33

On her 2nd jump the rope flew out of her hands and whacked Arizona on the back of his head.

Arizona was not amused. He snatched the skipping ropes from us and SLAMMED out of the house.

MONDAY MORNING May 19th 8.25am →

Never would I think that I could ever be ~~DESPARATE~~ DESPERATE to go to school, but I actually am! I've been dressed and ready for ages.

The whole of yesterday afternoon Vanilla and Mum floated round the house, wafting stinky candles and ~~insense insens~~ incense all over the place. I ~~practikly~~ practically suffocated 5 times!

OOOW YA POOYA CHINGG NICARAGA MINGA CHA LA RINGA...

PLUS I've now got to suffer 2 of them chanting, instead of just 1. And they seem to be in competition to go on the longest and loudest.

Then there's the wind chimes. → They keep you awake all night, and then you keep ~~aciderlty~~ accidentally crashing into them when you go up or downstairs.

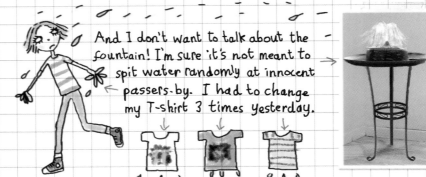

And I don't want to talk about the fountain! I'm sure it's not meant to spit water randomly at innocent passers-by. I had to change my T-shirt 3 times yesterday.

PLUS it's impossible to remember where anything is any more because all the furniture's moved.

DING DONG! Ooh - must be Keira at the door. HOORAY!

## 15 MINUTES LATER

## I DON'T BELIEVE IT!

I am now ~~offish~~ officially a prisoner!

Vanilla got to the front door before me and <u>sent</u> Keira <u>away</u>! She said that the ~~constelah konstell~~ constellations are not ~~orspish orspicious~~ auspicious for me to go to school today!

When I said...   (What's that in English?)   they just sent me back to my room.

I DON'T HAVE A ROOM!

UPSTAIRS, HYPPOLITA - NOW!

Squeak    Hoot    Whine    Click    Honk    Hoooot

So here I am, back in the wardrobe, ~~smolder~~ smouldering.
Which means stomping around loudly, banging drawers
shut, and slamming the door a lot.

But I don't think they can hear
anything above the ~~WALE~~ WHALE SONG
Vanilla has put on the CD player.

And I can honestly say, _nothing_ sounds
less like a song than whales hooting
at each other. But Vanilla says it
expresses —

> The Harmony of
> the Universe!

Yeah-right.

Anyway I'm now lying on my mattress, plugged into
some _decent_ music on my mp3 player (AXEKID) trying to
come up with a strategy.

## MY STRATEGIES

1. ESCAPE (easy in movies but scary in real life)
2. REVENGE (destroy the WHALE SONG CD)
3. SEND SOS TO KEIRA (but not sure how
   that would help)
4. GET RID OF VANILLA (YES!! But HOW???)
5. GET MY ROOM BACK (YES!! But HOW???)

37

And none of these strategies are going to help with the bigger problem of...

... **CELEBRITY HOME WATCH** featuring MY MUM!

The thought of it makes me feel too sick to ~~contamplate~~ contemplate.

Clearly trying to contemplate is ~~exorsting~~ exhausting, which is why I must have dropped off, and got all tangled up with my headphones.

It's not easy untangling wires when there's a really annoying BANGING going on outside your door...

BANG
BANG
BANG

... Actually **on** your door.

What?

Hyppolita – Serenity seems to be evading you. Now compose yourself and come downstairs to join your mother and me, as there is something we wish to share with you...

OH NO! Please not one of those horrible burnt seed bakes that Vanilla keeps trying to feed me...

I'm not hungry.

I'm not offering you food, child. Just move your feet and get downstairs... in a calm and joyful way of course.

38

Of course they are, Arabella, Golden One, but they are coming to the house, and Hyppolita lives here... so we need to prepare her.

Prepare me?

Hyppolita, will you please shut your mouth and try to look like an intelligent child. Do go on, Vanilla...

Hyppolita, as you know I consulted my charts...

I've seen these - they look a bit like star maps

...and I found that the constellations forbid you to leave home today...

I have no idea how she worked that one out - she seemed to spend much more time gazing into the distance than studying the chart

...Too many Tigers of Torment!

Tigers of Torment? In Highgate?

A metafor metaff metaphor, Polly, innocent one, a metaphor for the dangerous shar—

The dangerous shar?

Is she ever going to speak in a language that a person can understand?

The SHA...·S·H·A· is the bad energy, child! And·it is lurking ~~ominus~~ ~~aminers~~ ominously outside... so it would be best if you remained in your room, as that would be safest...

Er-I don't have a room-

...But if for some reason you do need to leave your room, and you encounter a TV personality -just leave any talking to your mother or me. Children can be-er-easily tricked, so it would be best (for your SPIRITUAL health) to simply smile and avoid conversation. Your spiritual health is our only concern of course.

Vanilla, Vanilla, Vanilla, you're in danger of losing focus on the most important thing!

The most important thing?

**ME** of course! Now what time is it?

41

Arabella, honeyed one, you know time is a borjwuh ~~corsept~~ concept. Time is just the human ~~ekwiv~~ equivalent of —

no idea what this means

Yes, yes, Vanilla, it is, it is, but the TV people are coming at 10.30. What time is it now?

Vanilla looked like she was about to waft on for another half an hour, so I knew someone had to put Mum out of her misery.

Twelve minutes past–

Twelve minutes past **WHAT**, Hyppolita? **Do** try to convey information when you mumble.

Twelve minutes past TEN.

VANILLA! Wardrobe – Now!

Roughly translated that sentence meant ...

Come on, Vanilla, it's time to strew clothes, hats, scarves, shoes and make-up all over Polly's few but well-loved possessions.

— DIAGRAM —

Me in a corner trying to avoid shoe missiles as she rejects outfit after outfit

But Arabella - green is the ~~orsp~~ auspicious colour for today. I have checked all my charts, the tea-leaves, the roons, and tarrow ...

must look up what all these are

But Vanilla - I look like a ~~joradis~~ jaundiced turkey!

Oh Luminous Lighted One — you positively glow in that colour. And it ~~orgers~~ augurs so well! The day will be a great success. Trust me.

In my opinion, people who say this are always the ones you need to be most suspicious of.

* Especially when they are called Vanilla.

* Especially when they are trying to convince your mum that she doesn't look putrid in the dress she's wearing.

There's the doorbell so the green had better be ~~orspish~~ auspicious.

43

## LATER

Vanilla has gone down to open the door, ordering me to...

STAY HERE.

Mum has shoved on her impossible-to-walk-in puke-green heels, and tottered down → the stairs after her, banging her head and swearing as she smashed into the wind chimes.

I took this with my phone

Of course I wasn't going to stay in that room. For many reasons...

① Because it isn't MY room and is not a place any normal person would want to spend her time.

② Because a person can't faithfully accurately record the truth if she's stuck in her mum's wardrobe.

③ I wanted to see what was going on!

As the front door opened Mum arrived downstairs, spread her arms and sang —

Welcome to my abode —

A girl with a clipboard shuffled in.

Mum ignored her, and waited (arms still spread) by the door.

The girl, who had been walking towards the kitchen, turned round...

...Ahem— Ms Diamonte, shall we make a start?

Mum frowned and walked through the front door and a little way down the path. Then she came back into the house.

Er Ms Diamonte?..

Mum stood there, mouth twitching.

45

Lucy decided that the only way she would be able to convey any information to my mum would be to speak very slowly...

Well, Ms Diamonte... I-am-Lucy-the-Programme's-assistant-producer. I-have-come-to-do-a-drawing-of-the-house—

I nearly fell over the banister taking this photo

A drawing of the house? How on earth is that going to help them make a programme? Are you mad, child?

Well-it will be a sort of diagram, so they know where all the rooms are, and they can plan shots. Toby, the producer, will be here in a few minutes I expect, to ask you a few questions...

So when are the crew getting here?

In a day or so. We don't have any leeway on this one...

...What with ~~Hump~~ Humphrey Hamilton dumping us in the lurch by pulling out at the last minute... and then having to find someone — <u>anyone</u> who'd do it at such short notice...

May I give you a little advice, Lucinda dear?

Er- Lucy, Ms Diamonte.

If you are fond of your tongue, I suggest you place it firmly at the back of your mouth, and keep it there. Then, perhaps you can get on with your drawings and ~~Vake~~ Vacate my house.

Lucy's eyes widened in bewildered shock, but she got her pencil out and started scribbling.

Mum turned and strode back up the stairs, crashing, of course, into the windchime on her way.

Vanilla hurried after her.

I had to dive back into the wardrobe and lie on my bed, like I'd been there all along.

As soon as Mum got in here she threw her impossible-to-walk-in puke-green shoes towards the door...

They narrowly missed Vanilla's head as she eased herself inside.

Arabella, Cherished One— remember your inner bliss! Breathe. Centre yourself.

Eventually Vanilla got her calmed down, which was just as well because Lucy had found her way up the stairs. The windchimes alerted us.

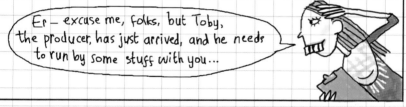

Er — excuse me, folks, but Toby, the producer, has just arrived, and he needs to run by some stuff with you...

Mum put her shoes back on and clomped down the stairs, trailed by Vanilla.

...mutter... Run by some stuff... What on earth is she talking about? mutter...

I leaned over the banisters to watch.

49

51

## ABOUT AN HOUR LATER (12.14 pm)

They're leaving.

Nothing at all to report because I couldn't hear a thing, though everything looks sickeningly friendly.

While I've been cooped up in here waiting, I have decided to start a ~~Campane campain~~ campaign to get back to school. I just can't face a whole afternoon stuck in here with nothing but my diary, Mum, Vanilla, the chanting and ~~insents incents~~ incense.

## 1.00 PM

The campaign has become even more urgent since Vanilla's lunchtime bean and black mushroom stew...

slime trail

murky sloppy blackness

un-identifiable lump

It was, in fact, while staring at the stew that <u>INSPIRATION</u> struck. Well it was probably <u>DESPERATION</u> actually. Black slop would make anyone desperate for an escape plan.

Do eat up, Polly.

Mmm— delicious.

THIS WAS MY INSPIRATION ← (It involves ~~brilliant sichology psit~~ psychology)

I suddenly realized that instead of whining...

When can I go back to school?

...and getting no answer whatsoever...

totally ignoring me

... I needed to take a different approach...

USE THE LANGUAGE OF THE ENEMY!

So I said...

Vanilla, are the constells favourable for me to go to school this afternoon?

She actually stopped slürping soup and looked at me!

Then she did the Vanilla smile.

Hyppolita, dear innocent! You mean constellations! Perhaps it would do no harm to do a reading...

And that's how I found out about THE ~~TARROW~~ TAROT.

## TAROT CARDS

It seems that Tarot Cards are another of Vanilla's
<u>IMPORTANT LIFE-COACH TOOLS</u>

But they don't have **spades** and **hearts** and stuff
like that on them.

They have weird pictures. ——>

Vanilla cleared away the sickening soup plates and put
5 of these cards down
on the table really slowly
in front of me.
Then she just sat there.

*Am I meant to pick them up, or something?*

helpful

*Shhh!*

bad-tempered

So I just sat there staring at the cards too. They
had horrible names- like HANGED MAN and
THE FOOL, and I had just decided that Vanilla
was probably a witch (of the Roald Dahl kind, rather
than the Harry Potter kind) when she stood up.

*Yes all right, Hyppolita- the energies appear reasonably
favourable. Perhaps you can go to school this afternoon.*

## YES!!!

54

## TUESDAY ● 20th May ● 8.30 am

## THE GOOD NEWS

Vanilla and Mum want to spend the day preparing for the TV crew at a Health Farm, and <u>LUCKILY</u> the constellations are favourable for me to go to school.

## THE BAD NEWS

Vanilla is making me wear a <u>HORRIFIC</u> necklace which she calls an amulet.

Its job is to ward off <u>evil</u>!

Ward off <u>friends</u> would be a better description.

I've learnt my lesson though. I just said –

Thank you, Vanilla.

All I have to do is stuff it inside my school shirt when I get out the door.

Don't know what I'm going to do about a note for Miss Pugitt, but <u>NO WAY</u> am I asking for one.

Keira's here – gotta go!

## TUESDAY NIGHT
## SOME REALLY ANNOYING NEWS

Harry Heathcliffe and two of his friends were lying in wait for Keira and me when we got to the front door.

And they walked behind us all the way to school.

AGHH! Has Harry Heathcliffe found out Mum's an actress? How will I ever keep Celebrity Home Watch a secret at school now???

BUT today wasn't ALL totally bad...

## SOME REALLY GOOD NEWS

1) When I got into school, Robbie Kildaire in my class said –

> Hi, Poll, are you better?

I _can't_ believe he spoke to me. He's _so_ cool!
   and

2) I got to spend the evening at Keira's, as Mum and Vanilla couldn't get back from the health farm till about 9pm.

## WEDNESDAY MORNING 9 am

I don't believe it! She wouldn't let me go to school again! I said in my sweetest voice –

> But Vanilla, I'm wearing the amulet, what possible evil can get me?

And she just shook her head, and pointed at the stupid ~~tarrow~~ tarot cards.

> Look, Hyppolita–how can I let you go out there with the **Ten Swords of Doom** _and_ **The Tower** on the table? It would be criminal!

But isn't it against the law to stop me going to school?

What do I care of Man's Laws? The Laws of the Universe are much more important! And don't worry- your time away from school won't be wasted. I have many books, which you will find much more informative than all that nonsense they teach you at school!

She wafted out and then wafted back in with this heavy, dusty book:

THE CONSTELLATIONS
The Believer's Guide to Life's True Journey and the Spirit's Mystical Path
by Madame Charla Tan

And as a special treat I'll let you listen to my Whale Song CD.

GREAT! What better way to spend a morning?

Obviously I wasn't going to read one of her mad books, or listen to that awful CD. So I've had a fair bit of time to fill in my diary.

PLUS — I managed to sneak the Ten of Swords and the Tower from the pack... Which means when she reads the cards tomorrow they won't stop me going to school! Cunning, eh?

**TEN of SWORDS**

**THE TOWER**

I'm sticking them here for safe-keeping

Oh NO! Mum and Vanilla are coming! Better pretend to be reading.

<u>NEAR DISASTER</u>  Vanilla saw my diary lying on the bed and asked what it was!!!

Er. it's a notebook...to -er- jot down - er-important new facts from your-er-wonderful book!

May the Mystical Lights be praised! A Spiritual breakthrough!

ROUGH TRANSLATION
I'll believe any old rubbish the girl talks

60

Vanilla and Mum have come to the wardrobe to sort out The Outfit For Today because this is offish officially F. Day. ← filming day
Vanilla wants Mum to wear white.

White will attract the right Chakra

(Of course I don't know what she's talking about, and I'm beginning to suspect that she doesn't either)

Mum is resisting...

Don't be ridiculous, Vanilla darling— I'll look like a bride! I think the Pink!

No, no, Arabella, the pink will excite the **SHA** and that will be very morspish inauspicious.

They compromised on yellow.

Mistake in my opinion.

This particular outfit makes Mum look like a banana.

But she was in it, and the doorbell was ringing, and I was keeping my mouth shut.

Coming!

Again Mum (in impossible-to-walk-in yellow heels) tottered down the stairs, crashed into the windchime and opened the door.

I have NEVER seen her so ignored.

Is this even a word?

I watched as the TV crew started putting all the furniture more or less the way we had it before Vanilla arrived.

She was ~~SMAOLDRING~~ ~~SMOLEDRING~~ SMOULDERING

While the house was being rearranged, Lucy (the AP) ~~corshus~~ cautiously approached my mum.

Er- Ms Diamonte, do you think I could ask you one or two questions?

I thought Charlie Bonnyface, the Celebrity Home Watch presenter, would be interviewing me.

Oh he will be, on the final shoot-day! I just need to get some info to help him with his questions. Is that OK?

Surely he can come up with his own questions?

Tee hee! Oh, presenters never write their own questions!

Mum does <u>not</u> like people who laugh at her. Unless she's in a comedy. Then she doesn't like people who don't.
But THIS was definitely not a comedy.
    She turned to the producer.

TOBIAS! I can't imagine you thought this twelve-year-old would be up to the job of interviewing ME?

Why don't you just leave us to make the programme, Arabella, love? We have done this before a few times...

Barnaby - we're going to need a cover on the mic when we record Arabella...she's so-um-vocally-er-powerful...

...Oh, and Arabella - Lucy happens to be one of our best APs, so I suggest you sit down together at that table and get going. Time is money, as they say-

No, Barnaby - the big one...

Surely Mum wasn't going to stand for this?
She'd have to throw them out now!

She stood in a frozen pose of FURY for a few
moments, certain that
someone would come
to her rescue.

But nobody did.
Not even Vanilla...
(who seemed to be →
ignoring everyone.)

## LATER

They started filming at lunch time. 'Just act normal', Toby said.

How marvellous to be
able to commune with
my Public—
Hyppolite! Elbows!

Ah yes...
I am utterly DEVOTED
to my dahling viewers...

mouth open in shock

...POLLY!
My public is
not interested
in the
contents
of your
mouth...

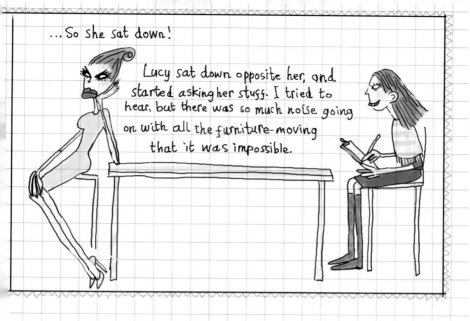

... So she sat down!

Lucy sat down opposite her, and started asking her stuff. I tried to hear, but there was so much noise going on with all the furniture-moving that it was impossible.

...Please SHUT IT! Now where was I...

me, working out how I can pretend to eat this gruesome gluey gunk without GAGGING

...The nation and I — Polly, that mung bean is on its third circuit round your plate — just put it in your mouth and SWALLOW!

It clearly wasn't quite what Toby had in mind.

Arabella, love, I've got a great idea! A DINNER PARTY! Here! Tonight! You could invite that actor, Daniel Hopkins - he's one of your mates, isn't he? And how about Nigel Dillane, the theatre director? Ooh - and Chelsea Doyle, that gorgeous young actress who played your daughter in that comedy last year?

DANIEL HOPKINS (torn from Mum's old copy of CHAT)

Actor Daniel Hopkins was at the ceremony presenting the best actor award to hot newcomer Jason Lyle.

CHELSEA DOYLE! She's- -er- out of the country!

Actually - She's rehearsing at Channel 4.

Well - I don't have her number -

Luckily I do! I can text her now!

Oh - and don't worry about cooking. The TV company will get food in.

Toby's thought of EVERYTHING! He must have guessed that NO ONE would eat here if they thought Mum had anything to do with the cooking.

Without another word, Mum stood up and left the room.
← Vanilla followed.

I sat there alone, trying to chew something unchewable, while the whole crew watched me silently.

What d'ya reckon they're doing?

Probably gone to check the ~~roons~~ ~~rhunes~~ runes.

The RUNES?

Yeah! Those weird stones with strange patterns that Vanilla keeps throwing.

She really uses RUNES? Come on, guys, let's see if we can get some footage!

And they all trooped out, leaving me free to chuck away the lunch remains.

It is now 1.15pm.

If I sneak out in the next few minutes, I could make it back to school in time for the afternoon...

But if I was to stay, I might ~~purswade~~ persuade Mum that this Celebrity Home Watch thing is an altogether <u>BAD IDEA</u>.

I've just peeked into the living room. The whole crew are arranged around Vanilla (who is throwing her stones as gracefully as a person throwing stones can).

CAMERA

Stagey gasp at camera

Oh! THE DREAD DRAGONS OF DESPOND! AH HHH!

Mum, determined to get some of the attention

Vanilla! This must mean that it will be inauspicious for me to throw a dinner party tonight! Am I right?

CAMERA

thoughtful gaze at camera

You know what, Arabella? I need some time briefing the crew for the filming tonight so we might slip off now and get back here for 5pm. Which means you can both **replenish!** OK? ~~Chow Ciaw~~ Bye for now!

The crew have all gone now, leaving Mum and Vanilla to do their ~~competative~~ competitive chanting.

NIKAAWAWA CHONGGG OOYAKA WAKAHACK AJARRA

I have 3 hours and 17 minutes to come up with a plan... or - slip off to school.

4.30pm

OK - I'm not very proud of this but I just thought maybe if my brain was stimulated with maths or DT (or Robbie Kildaire) I might suddenly come up with a strategy. So I - er - sneaked off to school.

Got there just in time. Said I'd been feeling sick (which was not a lie) and I forgot my note (which obviously was).

Had quite a good afternoon actually:

| WEDNESDAY PM |
|---|
| ENGLISH |
| ENGLISH |
| MUSIC |

my second favourite subject <u>and</u> **Robbie Kildaire** is in my set!

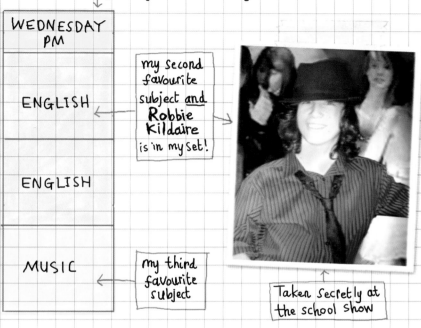

Taken secretly at the school show

my third favourite subject

No maths though. Which could be why I still don't have a plan...

And the crew will be here any minute.

Plus Mum and Vanilla have ~~barakad~~ ~~barrac~~ ~~barricaded~~ shut me out of my room as they're <u>both</u> trying on clothes.

I don't think I can take much more of this. Oh NO! The doorbell...

LATER (6.43pm)

The evening has not started well.

Toby and the crew arrived at 5pm and set up the lights and cameras.

Mum didn't come down for ages, as she kept changing her mind about clothes.

I just hung over the banisters watching all the food arrive, and the crew running around. ↓

Then Nigel Dillane (the theatre director) arrived.

Halloo, darlings!

I called Mum.

Chelsea! So glad you could make it - What a shame you didn't have time to go home and change.

I'm so sorry, Arabella! I didn't realize it was a FORMAL dinner!

Don't be silly, Chelsea - you look sensational

## I DON'T BELIEVE IT!

Chelsea Doyle plays **JADE** in **SISTERS** !!!

my favourite TV programme

And she's here in my house!!!

And she looks _even_ better in real life.

Taken secretly with my phone!

A bit of Daniel Hopkins

OK, everyone - that arrival scene was great -

We all turned to see Toby, Freddy and Jim had been filming.

But we need to shoot it again. Arabella - your dress is reflecting the light and bleaching out, so you'll just have to slip on something else...and you three - wait behind that tree - we'll go again!

JUST SLIP ON SOMETHING ELSE! Doesn't he realize that outfit took hours to put together? I didn't dare look at Mum's face. This HAD to be the final straw. Surely?

She turned silently and went upstairs. I crept after her, and listened at the door.

Sonia Snootwhistle! NO I CANNOT HOLD - Sonia! There is absolutely NO WAY I'm going to continue with this ridiculous sharard! The man's a buffoon! And he's JUST TOLD ME TO CHANGE MY CLOTHES! No, Sonia! I appreciate that, Sonia! But of course not. A COUPLE MORE DAYS COULD KILL ME! ... Do you think so?.. REALLY?.. Well perhaps- just for you... I love you too, darling ... All right! (phone down) Tra la la la la la La la!

Is that like the game?

Happy Singing?!!

What did Sonia say?     BUM! BUM! BUM!     77

# A BIT LATER (8·17 pm)

Well they've finally got through THE ARRIVAL OF GUESTS!
Poor Nigel, Daniel and Chelsea had to arrive 3 times before Toby
was happy. And each time they got a bit less enthusiastic.
I'm sure if I was a grown-up I'd have decided that NO dinner
was worth it.

Anyway by this time we were all STARVING. And we still
weren't ~~aloud~~ allowed to sit down and eat. We had to
MILL AROUND and talk to each other.

Vanilla ~~smolder~~ smouldering
in a corner.

The food was cold by the time we got it, but anything was better than Mum's cooking so I was NOT complaining. I just started ~~shuvell~~ shovelling it before anyone could say CUT.

After the first course, Mum was definitely back in a good mood...

...and had started telling some of her theatre stories...

— and I just told him frankly —

... when Barnaby (the sound man) suddenly waved his hands around...

...Darling-this is the last time —

OK-can you hold it there, Arabella? The ~~mike~~ mic isn't picking up properly...

People <u>DO</u> <u>NOT</u> interrupt Mum mid-flow...

Arabella, you need to know that you've got a teeny piece of spinach...

Chelsea was only trying to be helpful, but sorrowfully, this just sealed her fate.

Chelsea- how very kind of you to tell me, and with such familiarity! Almost as though you were family! Obviously I shall have to go and deal with it straight away...

Mum stood up from the table with her wine glass, swayed slightly, and somehow managed to stumble next to Chelsea's chair, tipping the contents of her glass all down Chelsea's front.

Oh what a clumsy accident! Silly, silly me!

Chelsea, you're SOAKED! Arabella- have you got anything Chelsea could change into?

Of course not! We're completely different sizes! Maybe something of Polly's? Hyppolita-take Chelsea upstairs and find some sort of garment... and spend as long as you like!

Me? Lend something to CHELSEA DOYLE??!!! But what?
I only have jeans and shorts, and she's way taller than me... Help!

15 MINUTES LATER

It turns out that Chelsea looks great in ANYTHING! She's borrowed a pair of my shorts, and a vest top.

WOW!

The reaction of everyone in the room... well, everyone except Mum and Vanilla

AT THE DINNER TABLE

I've brought my notebook down with me, so I can give a minute-by-minute account of the dinner — and at the same time avoid having to talk to anyone.

Uh-oh! Vanilla has just stood up.

I'm sorry - but the Chakra around this table is very blocked. Some **bad** energy is SEEPING around the room. I need to cleanse it -

What - right now, Vanilla?

Absolutely right now! It will only get worse otherwise.

I am beginning to feel <u>really</u> sick— especially when I see Toby and Freddy's faces.

Vanilla has disappeared, and we all wait in silence.

She's back... with wind chimes → and some ~~incents~~ ~~insens~~ incense.

WOOO, YUCKA··CHUKKA ··· AHRAYAH···

Now she's chanting and beating the wind chimes with a teaspoon. 83

I was just about to sit down when Vanilla put her head round the door

Hyppolita, infant one—I really think the land of slumber calls.

What is she on about?

Bedtime!

spine-chilling smile

Now I am **OUTRAGED!** Not because I wanted to stay in that room but because I have just been sent to bed like a kid, by an insane person who isn't even my mother, in front of Chelsea Doyle, and who knows how many TV viewers, many of which go to my school.

I walk out of the room with as much ~~dignerty~~ dignity as a person in my situation can (not much).

IN BED

I can hardly write, I am in such a state of **FURY** and ~~DISPAIR~~ DESPAIR. I will **NEVER** speak to Vanilla again.

85

There is definitely a strange atmosphere in the house today. Not just between me and Vanilla (I have NOT forgotten last night) but also between Mum and Vanilla.

And I'm totally sure that Mum's bad mood with Vanilla is NOTHING to do with LOYALTY to me. LOYALTY to her own flesh and blood is a virtue I don't think my mum has heard of.

What happened after I went to bed?

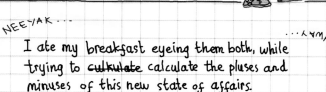

I ate my breakfast eyeing them both, while trying to ~~culkulate~~ calculate the pluses and minuses of this new state of affairs.

NIKAW...DRONE... DRONE... NEE-YAK...

SHWAY... BLAH...FEN... BLAH... AROO...

## PLUSES +

1) Vanilla will have to leave.

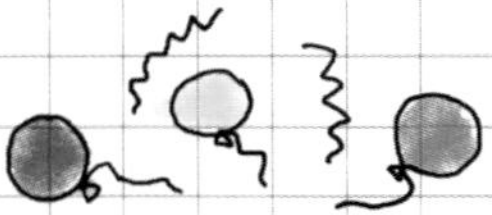

2) Which means she'll take away —

    (a) her Wind chimes. YES!

    (b) her ~~Tarrow~~ Tarot Cards. YES!!

    (c) her ~~Roons~~ Runes. YES!!!

    (d) her Fountains. YES!!!!

    (e) her Eggs. YES!!!!!

    (f) her Tigers of TORMENT. YES!!!!!!

3) I'll get _my_ room back. YES! **YES!** **YES!**

## MINUSES −

1)

I can't think of _a_ _single_ minus!

So how can I make TOTALLY SURE that things don't improve
between them?

87

Toby is OUTRAGED! <u>Nobody</u> postpones filming. He starts making frantic phone calls...

What about the schedule?.. Yes, I guess I could start filming him today, but I'd need two clear days... fine...

Right. We're giving you two days' break, then we'll be back Saturday to wrap up— <u>whatever</u> the Dogs of Doom are doing.

And out they crash.

I still have time to get to...

Hyppolita, my vulnerable one, where are you going?

School?

But where is the AMULET? You MUST NEVER leave home without it! What <u>were</u> you thinking?

I am **sooo** relieved that she's not stopping me from going, I dash upstairs and grab it from the floor.

Vanilla is guarding the front door, but lets me pass.

FREEDOM!!!

DOUBLE FREEDOM—

I'm so late Harry Heathcliffe has already gone!

4.30 ish pm

☁ THE BAD NEWS ☁

Mum and Vanilla seem to be utterly friends again (I should have stayed home).

They've booked a <u>bonding</u> day at the health club tomorrow.

Massage is so good for the -

-Chi

☀ THE GOOD NEWS ☀

I get to go to school and Keira's again.

FRIDAY Morning 23rd May 8.30am

I sensibly trot downstairs wearing the amulet.

Vanilla looks suitably pleased

Polly! I really believe that the amulet is actually improving your spiritual health. See how much more calm and lovely you have become.

Big ~~mean~~ insincere grin

Mmm—Yes, Vanilla.

Yeah, right!

LATER 9.30pm

THE GOOD THINGS ABOUT TODAY

1 Double Art! My totally best subject! And we're designing CD covers. I'm doing an AXE KID design.

My Axe Kid Badge

AXE KID

2 English (with Robbie Kildaire). We both agreed that this is a totally brilliant book, though really scary.     →

The Boy
in the
Striped
Pyjamas

JOHN BOYNE

But Joe Butcher said it wasn't scary at all. He totally didn't see the point. And it was boring. Quite a lot of the class agreed with him.

3 Went home with Keira. I really like Keira. I almost told her about Celebrity Home Watch. But then I just couldn't.

THE BAD THINGS ABOUT TODAY

Harry Heathcliffe and his horrible friends were ~~definat~~ definitely lying in wait for me to leave the house this morning. Luckily I got the amulet tucked in, so they just ~~consen~~ concentrated on my other failings.

Axe kid cap

Like the ~~suttle~~ Subtle colours Polly-Parrot-Price!

SNORT!

Aw! Not wearing your HOT PE kit today, then! Shame!

Snigger!

She returned with a serene smile.

Happily, the cards foretell beauty and light outside. Arabella, Enlightened One, you will need to wear blue...

Blue? But—

Come, my dove, we must find something suitable...

While Mum and Vanilla disappeared to the wardrobe, Toby and the team huddled.

Blah, blah, wind shield mikes mics, blah, blah, check in the van, blah...

Then Toby made about a thousand phonecalls, while I sat in a corner and caught up on events, until Vanilla and Mum emerged.

How about meeting us there?

Yeah, 10.30 sounds good.

We were all finally leaving the house when Vanilla gasped.

Hyppolita - AMULET!

GRRR!

I reluctantly trudged upstairs and put it on. There was absolutely NO POINT trying to hide it, because that would only cause another scene, so I had to suffer the fashion humiliation of wearing it over my T-shirt, and walk down the stairs towards Freddy the cameraman.

As if this morning wasn't bad enough, Harry Heathcliffe and gang were hanging around. BUM BUM BUM!

They stared as we all trooped out.

Now all hope of keeping this quiet was definitely OVER. They were already on their mobiles...

Thankfully we were going off to an unknown location.

I stupidly left my diary upstairs when I got the amulet - so borrowed this from Lucy, who's quite nice actually. The reason it's so damp and crumpled will become clear.

Mum, me and Vanilla got into Mum's car. Toby and the crew got into a blue van, and we set off.

It was only a 10-minute ride, but I felt quietly confident that we hadn't been followed —

**Oh NO!**

When we got out of the car, Mum charged off towards the lake, but Toby made her stop, so that Freddy could get in front of her to film her progress. To stay far enough ahead he had to run <u>backwards</u>! (Not easy while holding a camera!)

But Frederick, you won't know where I'm going!

Trust me, Arabella, I've done this before!

I have probably walked in the park a million times, and I've never found __walking__ difficult before. But what with Freddy pointing a camera at me, and the various innocent bystanders watching, I suddenly found it incredibly hard to just put one foot in front of the other!

Then there was the problem of my deranged arms and hands. What do I do with my hands normally? Because right now they seemed to be hanging there like a pair of __floppy ping-pong bats__. Not to mention my head, which had started to feel way too heavy for my neck.

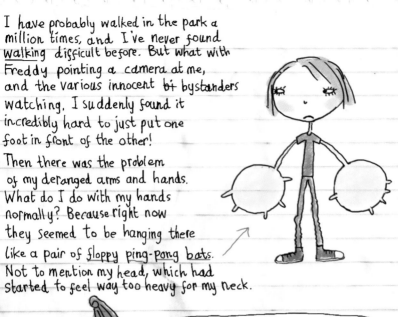

Do try not to slouch, Polly-doodle! Straight and tall, chin to chest!

Thanks, Mum. That really helped.

As if things weren't bad enough, Vanilla wafted towards us and closed in, until I was a pink slice of girl-sandwich.

Fortunately, annoyance with Vanilla took my mind off the ping-pong bats and concrete head, and somehow my feet managed to carry me right up to the lake.

Unfortunately Freddy...

Aghh!

...got there just ahead of us.

Watch out—

While Freddy tried to dry off, we all gathered by the boat-hire booth.

Waiting for us surrounded by fans was Charlie Bonnyface, Celebrity Home Watch Presenter

With a little flick, Mum replaced Vanilla's hand on Charlie's shoulder with her own.

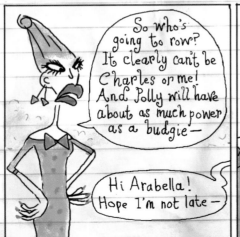

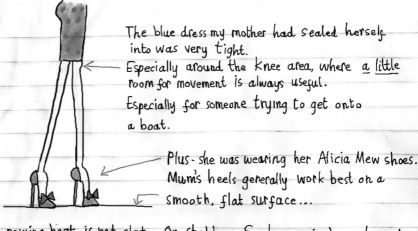

The blue dress my mother had sealed herself
into was very tight.
Especially around the knee area, where <u>a little</u>
room for movement is always useful.
Especially for someone trying to get onto
a boat.

Plus- she was wearing her Alicia Mew shoes.
Mum's heels generally work best on a
smooth, flat surface...

A rowing boat is not flat. Or stable. So her arrival on board
was not exactly smooth...

105

As soon as we set off, Charlie got going.

Arabella Diamonte, this park is a favourite haunt of yours, I understand.

Yes, Charles, we've been coming here since Pollypoops was in nappies! Haven't we, Muffin?..

How could she do this to me? On camera?

As I looked around for an escape hatch, I spotted Harry Heathcliffe with a whole gang of kids from school, standing by the boathouse... waving.

Could things get any worse?

Yes.

...HAVEN'T WE, MUFFIN?

gulp...

In the space my answer was supposed to fill, Vanilla seized her moment—

Charlie- this park is ~~orspish~~ auspiciously placed on the site of an Ancient Druid Temple! You can positively feel the spiritual energy rising up through—

107

"Yes, Vanilla, I'm sure Charles would be delighted to get his history lesson LATER— but as I was saying—"

"Arabella, I think you might do well to shut your eyes for a moment, breathe deeply and slowly, and rebalance your chi! Your spiritual health—"

"VANILLA—You BABBLING BOLUS! Will you just shut your RIDICULOUS mouth for FIVE MINUTES and let me GET ON with this interview. And you're taking up SO MUCH of the boat that I can't even make EYE CONTACT with Charles. So for goodness sake— MOVE!"

Vanilla just sat there for a couple of seconds, blinking. Then she heaved herself forward and up.

This turned out to be a <u>very</u> <u>bad</u> idea, as the whole boat suddenly wobbled horrifically.

Mum ignored it.

"SWAP SEATS!"

"NO!"

Toby from the other boat

These were the last words I heard as I suddenly found myself whooshed off the boat.

AAGHH!

## SURPRISING FACT

When you find yourself unexpectedly tipped into the water, your brain seems to take a few seconds to notice.

And you'd think that once it _has_ noticed, it might switch on the 'LET'S SWIM TO SAFETY' response.

Unfortunately, mine just thought—

Whoa! This water's cold!

So I carried on sinking.

When my brain finally got round to the 'Let's swim to safety' thought, I was stuck.

The amulet had caught round some tree root and I couldn't undo it.

Change of paper represents extreme change of circumstance (I couldn't write under water!)

109

# RESCUE?!!

...then hauled me up to the surface.

By the time we got back to the boat, my mother was HYSTERICAL.

VANILLA- THIS IS ALL YOUR FAULT- IF YOU HAD-

That did it. Mum just started ranting furiously at Vanilla, totally ignoring the crowds of people watching from the shore.

RANT-SHOUT-SCREAM-BELOVED DAUGHTER-RANT.

She also ignored the fact that a camera was filming the whole scene.

And of course she totally ignored the fact that Chelsea and me were both freezing to death.

who has just saved my life

her BELOVED daughter

by Polly Price

# THE RESCUE   Episode 2

Luckily a safety boat had just motored up to us, and within a matter of seconds Chelsea and I were bundled on board, wrapped in tin foil and zooming off, away from the camera, my mum, and the crowds.

~~Heroicly~~ Heroically, they helped me peel off my wet clothes and wrapped me in warm, fluffy blankets and more silver foil. But I couldn't even say thank-you, because my teeth were chattering too much.

And then for some reason I started to cry. This was quite embarrassing.

ME
A TOTAL MESS!

leaking eyes →

chattering teeth

Chelsea was sooo cool though. She said it was probably just the body's response to getting warm. She even said she felt like crying. Then she gave me a hug and I started crying a bit more.

And then we both laughed.

112

Then I started worrying about how I was going to get home. I definitely couldn't leave looking like a baked potato.

Would Toby and the crew be waiting outside with cameras?

The thought of that made me start crying again.

silver foil →

Don't you worry, ducks, we've got some lovely warm, dry clothes for you both.

MY HEROES

Suddenly Mum came bursting in.

Oh Pollypoops - you're here! No thanks to Vanilla and her protective amulet! Anyway, she's packing her bags right now!

What about the crew?

Oh they've gone - We're finished with them now.

It was true! By the time we emerged there was no sign of Vanilla, the crew or the crowds of people.

WHAT A RELIEF! IT WAS UNDER!!!

## FRIDAY EVENING 20th June

Obviously it isn't actually over. There's still the programme to worry about. For the last 3 Fridays I've been walking around with a sickening feeling which gets to crisis point at exactly 7.15 pm.

Sickish · quite sick · really quite sick · considerably sick · very sick · Very very sick · Chuck-up time

1.15 · 2.15 · 3.15 · 4.15 · 5.15 · 6.15 · 7.15

Celebrity Home Watch

And for the last 3 Fridays, Celebrity Home Watch has always ~~feechered~~ featured <u>someone</u> else!
Tonight <u>will</u> ~~definate~~ definitely be the night — I just know it.

## 8.15 PM
NO!! Not on <u>again</u>! The RELIEF is <u>soooo</u> FANTASTIC!!!

## 9.00 PM
I'm not relieved any more. I'm already worrying about next week.
I wonder is Mum's actually been given <u>an</u> <u>actual</u> date?
I'm going to ask her...

## 10 PM
This is what she said...

Does this mean it's over?

Am I free???

Can I go on to lead a normal life????

SATURDAY 21st June 9.30am
Going round to Keira's today. Ellie and Jo are going too.

LATER 8.17pm
Just got back! Had a GREAT time.
We went to the park on our blades,
and Robbie Kildaire from my class
was there. And he came over
and said

Hi!

He even said

You're pretty fast
on your skates.

Not nearly as fast as him though.

I could have stayed at the park all day after that, but we had to get
back to Keira's for tea. Which was really, really good.

pizza

coke

chocolate
cake

cucumber

chips

Then we settled down on the sofa with some popcorn and watched **SISTERS** which was brilliant. ↓

Jade (Chelsea!) and Adonis started to fall in love...

...but then Jocasta found out and threatened to kill them both!

But Dominic (who is secretly in love with Jocasta) is trying to stop her!

It's sooo good! Obviously I was dying to tell everyone that Chelsea had been to my house, had worn my shorts, and had actually saved my life! But that would have meant telling them about Mum filming. So I couldn't.

Then Keira's dad said it was time to take me home.

Mum's busy chanting so I'm going to watch a bit of TV before bed.

I've had such a lovely day!

117

# My LIFE IS **DEFINITELY COMPLETELY TOTALLY** OVER.

OK- I switched on the TV, and Celebrity Hissy Fit was just starting.

(Oh good!) I thought happily as I settled down to watch Joe Capone pushing his way through a load of photographers.

Then **HORROR OF HORRORS-**

I am looking at our dining room, and sat round the table are Nigel Dillane, Daniel Hopkins, Chelsea Doyle, Vanilla, ME, and worst of all, MUM. →

Chelsea, how very kind of you to tell me, and with such familiarity...

Then Mum is tipping wine all down Chelsea's front! →

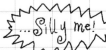

...Silly me!

But it's not over:

[Scene 2] Our Living Room

I'm missing, thankfully (must be after I was sent to bed). But I can see Daniel, Nigel, Vanilla and Chelsea (in my shorts and top).

Mum's in the middle of one of her theatre stories when Vanilla suddenly shrieks

Who left the door open? The Chi will escape, the Dragons of Doom will enter the –

Mum's face turns ~~pewse~~ PUCE!

VANILLA, you VAST, VAPID VAMPIRE –
How DARE you interrupt? Who do you think you are? Where do you think you are? What do you think you're here for? Well let me tell you! You're here to assist and smooth my life. NOT RUIN IT! And if you EVER shriek when I'm talking again I'll have you SERTIFIED!

Must look this up

119

AGGH! I can't take any more!

But the worst was still to come:

SCENE 3  The Park

# OH NO!...

...That's me falling out of the boat. On NATIONAL TV!

Could anything be more ~~humilliat~~ humiliating? Chelsea is first to react. The _only_ one to react actually...

Now Mum's face is filling the screen...

VANILLA! You repulsive TOAD of a woman! You've **snaked** your way into my life, **POISONED** us with your **disgusting** incense, ruled our lives with your stupid cards and stones, and Now...NOW look what you've done to my daughter! You are **EVIL** and **GROTESKQUE** and...

...As for **YOU LOT** -You **DISGUST** me! You'd rather carry on filming than rescue my child! And if you **DARE** to broadcast any of this on Celebrity Home Watch, I will **sue** you to ~~bankrupsie~~ **bankruptcy** and ~~ecstinxion~~ **extinction.**

Mum pushing the camera away

And that's it! The titles come up and I am stranded on the
armchair ~~parrolized~~ paralysed by

# DESPAIR

This is worse than anything I could have imagined.
This is beyond ~~enduerants~~ ~~endurants~~ unbearable.

# I CAN NEVER LEAVE THE HOUSE AGAIN!!!

## SUNDAY EVENING

Stayed in my room all day (apart from trips to the kitchen
for supplies).
Mum didn't even notice.
My mobile has been ringing
all day, but I've just been
letting it ring.

## MONDAY MORNING 9.30 AM

I told Mum I felt too sick to go to school (<u>not</u> a lie).
So I'm back in bed. I heard the doorbell, but just ignored
it. Thankfully Mum was chanting, so nobody answered it.

MONDAY 3PM

I am <u>sooo</u> **BORED**. How can I spend the rest of my life in my bedroom? I've totally run out of things to do.

Going to go downstairs. I can hear Mum on the phone in her Sanctum.

*Blah, blah, No! I mean it, Sonia! Blah blah!*

Perhaps I'll watch some TV.

<u>WHAT AM I THINKING???</u> I don't think I'll ever be able to watch TV again.

Hmmm...maybe now that I've experienced <u>true despair</u> I could write a poem about it.

Hey! I could become A POET!

Poets always lead tragic and solitary lives.

I would probably have to move to the country, as poets need to wander around in scenery.

Especially poets who don't want to be seen by people they know.

Tragic but brilliant expression

Lots of trees and scenic vistas

Long white wafty dress

123

# MY TRAGIC LIFE

A Poem by Polly Price
(aged nearly 12)

Alone in my room
With nothing to do
Except think how my life is doomed
The doors are locked ←
Time has stopped
I'm like a ship marooned. ←

They aren't really.
This is a ~~metafor~~ metaphor.
Miss Jordan (the English
Teacher) would be impressed.

~~Simatly~~ Simile! Probably
worth a House Point

The wind chimes are gone
My bedroom's my own
And glory should be mine
But now tragedy's struck
I'm so out of luck
That all I can do is ~~whine~~ pine.

Some people have normal mothers
Some people have lives full of sun
Some people get decent food for tea
Like sausages, chips and a bun ←

I couldn't think
of a better ~~fyme~~ rhyme

But mine is a life of the darkest gloom

## A BIT LATER

I was interrupted in my poetry by a banging on the window. I peeped out. Ellie, Keira and Jo had their faces pressed up against the glass.

Polly! You were on TV!

DUH!

Was **CHELSEA DOYLE** really in **YOUR HOUSE???**

Were those your shorts she was wearing?

Aggh! You are SOOO lucky!

Did she really save your life?

Polly — you've got to come to school tomorrow...

... EVERYONE wants to talk to you!

**TUESDAY 24th June**

Keira came over and made me go to school. I opened the door really ~~corshusly~~ cautiously, to check there was no sign of...

... PUBLIC ENEMY No. 1
(Harry Heathcliffe)

H. H.

LUCKILY the coast
was clear!

When I got to school it was UNBELIEVABLE!

Keira, Jo and Ellie went everywhere with me, cos they were so excited that they knew someone who'd been on TV!

Then when we went outside for break, <u>loads</u> of kids crowded round.

Robbie Kildaire

Hey, can I have your mum's autograph?

Can you get your mum to sign my schoolbag?

You were on TV!

That's her!

It looked like nobody was at all bothered by her ~~exefoostriating escfushiat~~ awfulness... Until HARRY HEATHCLIFFE strolled over.

I'm surprised you could bring yourself to show your face in school today...SNIGGER... If I was in your position I would have climbed under the nearest rock AND STAYED THERE!

Everyone around went really quiet... and then Robbie Kildaire (YES-<u>ROBBIE KILDAIRE</u>) came and stood beside me.

OK, Harry - I think some of us would quite like to see **YOU** climb under under a rock and stay there... SO WHAT ARE YOU WAITING FOR?

The whole playground went silent. Harry just stood gaping for a minute, and then ... SKULKED OFF!!!

# COULD MY LIFE GET <u>ANY BETTER</u>??!!!

**YES!** This arrived today!
↓

CHELSEA DOYLE

Monday 23rd June

Dear Polly,

Hope you've recovered from the boating adventure! I've only just got rid of the smell of pondweed from my hair!

I remembered that you said you watched SISTERS, so I thought you might like some tickets for the live recording?

Hope you can make it!

Love Chelsea x

I wonder if Robbie would like to come?

Robbie(!) ↑    Me ↑

Chelsea(!!!) ↑    Keira ↑

RAINBOW VALLEY PRODUCTIONS present:

# SISTERS

## C 5 TELEVISION STUDIOS

HAMMERSMITH    LONDON    W6 5TV

PRICE: **GUEST** MON 7 JULY 15.00

TICKET NO: JKO37Y

C 5 TELEVISION STUDIOS
HAMMERSMITH   LONDON   W6 5TV
PRICE: **GUEST** MON 7 JULY 15.00

my ticket ! ↑

Gold thread from Chelsea's Fight Costume

Chelsea gave me this! She wore it in the airplane scene

# CHELSEA & JASON?!

Spotted getting into a cab together, Chelsea Doyle (star of *Sisters*) and Oscar winning Jason Leary (*Dragon Slayer*) had spent a quiet evening in Margo's. Is Jason finally over his big break with Lois? Is Chelsea ready to settle down?

I can't believe Chelsea and Jason are together. Keira cut this out for me.

This is Chelsea's actual lipstick on a tissue. I sat next to her in her dressing room.

# The MOST secret and private page and Completely PRIVATE.

Amulet - this is the place where Chelsea cut it to save my life

# HISSY FIT TO END ALL HISSY FITS!

Arabella Diamonte gets a court injunction on her appearance in *Celebrity Home Watch*, but not before reams of pirate footage has been released.

Diamonte was the late choice celebrity for the show when Humphrey Hamilton pulled out for personal reasons.

Sources report that Ms Diamonte was one of the more challenging stars the company has had to work with, but presenter Charlie Bonnyface refused to comment.

*Celebrity Home Watch's* loss was *Celebrity Hissy Fit's* gain, and MCB4 reported unprecedented viewing figures when the show aired this week.

**Another chance to catch Arabella Diamonte on the *Celebrity Hissy Fit* repeat tonight at 8 pm on MCB4.**

R.K

An extremely PRIVATE poem
by Polly Price

Sometimes life is very hard
 With CERTAIN people about
Who force you into a cubpboard
Then **CHANT** incredibly loud

And then they RUIN your life
 By being **AWFUL** on TV
Not just any old programme
But one EVERYONE will see.

As if this isn't bad enough
There's the person I abhor ← Quite proud of
Who's greatest pleasure in life    this word - it
Is being mean to the girl next door.    means hate!

But ~~occasianly~~ occasionally goodness happens
And someone is very kind
 And also very handsome
A person with a brilliant mind

**A person** who is also brave
 A person I'd **be** happy to share
My packet of Refreshers with (if I had some)
A boy called ~~Robbie Kildaire~~

↖ Must remember
  to rub this out